Could you stop Josephine?

Stéphane Poulin

Tundra Books

My name is Daniel and last Sunday was my birthday.
My cat's name is Josephine and it was her birthday too.

"Let's go to the country for the day," my father said,
  "to visit your cousins."

"Can I take Josephine?" I asked.
"No," my father said. "Cats don't like cars."

I felt bad about leaving Josephine.
But when I saw the white farmhouse, I forgot all about her.

My aunt and uncle, my cousins Norman and John and their
    dog Cleo all came out to meet us.
We hugged and kissed, and Cleo barked.

We went into the house but Cleo kept barking.
I looked out the window.
Josephine was in the trunk of the car.
She had come all the way with us.

I went out to get her but she ran off.
Cleo ran after her.

I followed them to a field of cows.
Josephine ran under the gate.
I climbed over it.

She sat down under a big bull.
I looked at the big bull and the big bull looked at me.
"Come here, Josephine," I called.

But Josephine didn't come.
She ran off again.
She went through a hole into a little white shed.
I opened the door.

Out ran Josephine, then Cleo and then three little pigs.

Norman came to find me, just in time to catch the pigs.
I went after Josephine.

She ran into another field and hid under a tractor.
I bent down to look for her.
A cat ran out.
But it wasn't Josephine.
It was Norman's cat, Rupert.
Josephine was on top of the tractor.

Suddenly there was a big noise.
Josephine jumped down and ran.
A storm was coming.

"Josephine, stop! Don't be scared."

But Josephine didn't stop. She ran. Rupert ran. And Cleo ran after them both.

"Quick, Daniel," Norman yelled. "Get into the barn before the rain."

Norman and I sat in the barn and watched the storm.

Rain came down. Thunder roared. Lightning flashed.
It was a very big storm.

"Josephine is scared in storms," I told him.
"ALL animals are scared in storms," Norman said.

"Josephine doesn't like to get wet," I said.
"NO animal likes to get wet," Norman said.

"DUCKS like to get wet," I said.
"Ducks aren't animals," Norman said.

Then I saw Josephine.
She and Rupert were sitting high up on a beam watching us.

The storm ended.
Josephine was gone before I could stop her.

"I'll help you get her," Norman said.
I was glad he was with me.

Suddenly chickens and feathers flew everywhere.
Josephine ran out, then Rupert and then Cleo.

This time they crossed the road.
A farmer pointed to the wheat field.

The wheat was too tall for us to see anything.
"Josephine is really lost now," I said.

"You go that way," said Norman. "I'll go this way."

I went to the end of the field and stopped.
In front of me was a cliff. I looked down.
A train passed underneath. Beyond that was the river.
Where was Josephine?

Then I saw her.
She was sitting on the fence near me, stopped at last.
I grabbed her.

"Bad cat," I said. "You could have got hurt."
I held her tight all the way back.

Near the house, I saw them.
My father, my aunt, my uncle, Norman and John.
They were having a picnic.

"Happy birthday, Daniel," they called.
I was so surprised I dropped Josephine.
She ran off again.

"Never mind her," my father said. "Come to your party.
Then we'll all go and look for Josephine."

And that's what we did.
Only we couldn't find her.
Not with the cows. Not with the pigs. Not with the chickens.
Not in the wheat. Not even at the cliff by the railroad track.

The sun was going down
   when we got back near the house.
That's where we found the three of them,
   eating what was left of my party.

Then I remembered.
It was Josephine's birthday too.

To Francis

© 1988, Stéphane Poulin

Published in Canada by Tundra Books, Montreal, Quebec H3G 1R4

Published in the United States by Tundra Books of Northern New York, Plattsburgh, NY 12901

Distributed in the United Kingdom by Ragged Bears Ltd., Andover, Hampshire SP11 9HX

ISBN 0-88776-216-6 hardcover 10, 9, 8, 7, 6, 5, 4, 3, 2
ISBN 0-88776-227-1 softcover 10, 9, 8, 7, 6, 5, 4, 3, 2
Library of Congress Catalog Card Number 88-50260

Also available in French edition, *Pourrais-tu arrêter Joséphine?*
ISBN 0-88776-217-4 hardcover, 0-88776-228-X softcover
Library of Congress Catalog Card Number 88-50261

Canadian Cataloguing in Publication Data: Poulin, Stéphane. Could you stop Josephine? I. Title. PS8581.0846C69 1988 jC843'.54 C88-090130-6 PQ3919.2.P68C69 1988

The publisher has applied funds from its Canada Council block grant for 1988 toward the editing and production of this book.

The paintings from this book have been given an exhibition at the Shayne Gallery, Montreal.

Color transparencies and separations: TechnoColour Inc., Montreal

Printed in Belgium